Alexander Anteater's Amazing Act

by Barbara deRubertis • illustrated by R.W. Alley

THE KANE PRESS / NEW YORK

Alpha Betty's Class

Alexander Anteater

Bobby Baboon

Corky Cub

Dilly Dog

Eddie Elephant

Frances Frog

Gertie Gorilla

Hanna Hippo

Lana Llama

Izzy Impala

Jeremy Jackrabbit

Kylie Kangaroo

Maxwell Moose

Library of Congress Cataloging-in-Publication Data

deRubertis, Barbara.
Alexander Anteater's amazing act / by Barbara deRubertis ; illustrated by R.W. Alley.
p. cm. — (Animal Antics A to Z)
Summary: With help from his friends Anna and Albert, Alexander Anteater works on a
truly amazing acrobatic act for the talent show at Alpha Betty's school.
ISBN 978-1-57565-304-4 (lib. bdg. : alk. paper) — ISBN 978-1-57565-300-6 (pbk. : alk. paper)
[1. Talent shows—Fiction. 2. Acrobatics—Fiction. 3. Anteaters—Fiction. 4. Animals—Fiction.
5. Humorous stories.] I. Alley, R. W. (Robert W.), ill. II. Title.
PZ7.D4475Ale 2010
[E]dc22   2009024481

10 9 8 7 6 5 4 3 2 1

First published in the United States of America in 2010 by Kane Press, Inc.
Printed in Hong Kong
Reinforced Library Binding by Muscle Bound Bindery, Minneapolis, MN

Series Editor: Juliana Hanford
Book Design: Edward Miller

Animal Antics A to Z is a trademark of Kane Press, Inc.

www.kanepress.com

"Alexander Anteater, you do not look happy.
In fact, you look rather sad," said Alexander's dad.

Alexander began to wail.
"Next Saturday is the talent show at
Alpha Betty's school.
All the other kids have amazing acts.
But I can't do *anything*!"

"You could tap dance!" said Dad.

"But I can't dance *fast*!" said Alexander.

"You could play your banjo!" said Dad.

"But I can't play *fast*!" said Alexander.

"Well, I happen to know you can stand
on your hands," said Dad.

"Yes, I can do that," said Alexander.
"But that's not *amazing*."

"Use your imagination," said Dad.
"Maybe you can make it amazing."

Just then the doorbell rang.
It was Anna Anaconda.

"Wow!" she said when she saw
Alexander standing on his hands.
"You are an acrobat, Alexander!"

"I'm practicing for the talent show at Alpha Betty's school," said Alexander.

"But lots of kids can stand on their hands. I want to do something amazing."

"Can you do any acrobatic tricks, Anna?" Alexander asked.

Anna laughed. "Well . . . I can balance a tray of stacked glasses on my head!"

"Cool!" said Alexander.

He ran to the kitchen and came back with a tray
and six plastic glasses.
"Can you show *me* how to do that?" he asked.

"Absolutely!" said Anna.
She stacked the glasses on the tray.

Then she wiggled and waggled.
She swayed back and forth.

In no time flat, she was standing on her tail.

Alexander placed the tray of glasses on her head.

"Fantastic!" said Alexander and Dad.

The doorbell rang again.
This time it was Albert Alligator.

"Come in," said Alexander.
"We're doing acrobatic acts.

Anna can balance a tray of
glasses on her head.

I can stand on my hands.
What can you do, Albert?"

"I can stand on my head," said Albert.

"And I think I could balance that tray
of glasses on my tail."

In no time flat, Albert was standing on his head.

Alexander placed the tray of glasses on Albert's tail.

"Fantastic!" said Alexander, Anna, and Dad.

"It's too bad your pals aren't in your class, Alexander,"
said Dad. "Together, your talents are amazing!"

Alexander snapped his fingers. "That's it!" he said.
"I have an idea for a *new* acrobatic act!
But I'll need a lot of practice.
And I'll need your help," he told Anna and Albert.

"That's what pals are for!" they said.

Day after day, Anna and Albert helped
Alexander practice in his room.

The first day, Dad heard a loud *CRASH!*
"Alexander!" Dad called. "Are you okay?"

"Yes, Dad!" Alexander called back.
"But I'm glad we're using plastic glasses."

The next day, Dad heard a loud *SMASH!*
"Alexander!" Dad called.
"Are you okay?"

"Yes, Dad!" Alexander called back.
"But I may need some more
plastic glasses."

On the last day before the talent show,
Dad heard *bang . . . bang . . . bang . . . BANG!*
"Alexander!" Dad called. "Are you okay?"

"Yes, Dad!" Alexander called back.
"But may I please have more plastic glasses?"

Finally the big day came.
Alexander and his pals raced to
Alpha Betty's school.

Dad sat in the front row.
He waited for the talent show to begin.
What would Alexander *do*?

Alpha Betty happily rang a bell.

"Welcome to our talent show!" she said.
"Our class has *many* talents, as you shall see!"

One classmate sang. One tap danced.

One did magic tricks. One played a banjo.

Alexander was last. He was *very* excited.

"I will do an acrobatic act," he announced.
"My pals Anna and Albert will assist me."

Alexander stood on his hands.
Everyone clapped.

Anna placed a tray of stacked glasses
on Alexander's nose.
Everyone clapped and clapped.

Albert balanced a tray of stacked glasses
on Alexander's tail.
Everyone clapped and clapped and clapped.

Alexander smiled.

Then Anna and Albert stepped back.
Waaaaay back.

Albert put his hands over his ears.
Anna put her tail over her eyes.

Suddenly, Alexander *SPRANG* into the air.

The trays of glasses sailed up above his head.

He flipped over and . . .

BAM!

Alexander landed on his feet.

And he was balancing a tray of glasses on each hand!

Now everyone was standing up and cheering.
Dad and Anna and Albert were cheering loudest of all.

"Hooray for Alexander!" everyone chanted.
For Alexander Anteater's act was
absolutely *AMAZING!*

31

FUN FACTS

- Home: Central and South America
- Size: Up to 7 feet long—from the nose to the tip of the tail
- Weight: Up to 100 pounds
- Favorite foods: Anteaters use their sticky tongues to capture and eat ants, termites, and grubs. Yum!
- **Did You Know?** A giant anteater's tongue may be as long as 2 feet. No wonder they can eat as many as 30,000 ants in one day!

LOOK BACK

Learning to identify letter sounds (phonemes) at the beginning, middle, and end of words is called "phonemic awareness."

- The word *cap* has a *short a* sound. Listen to the words on page 6 being read again. When you hear a word that has the *short a*, clap and say the word.
- The word *snake* has a *long a* sound. Listen to the words on page 15 being read again. When you hear a word that has the *long a* sound, raise your hands and say the word.
- **Bonus!** Listen to page 14 being read again. When you hear a word that <u>begins</u> with a *short a* sound (like *Albert*), stand up! When you hear the next word that <u>begins</u> with a *short a*, sit down! (Continue until you've reached the end of the page.)

TRY THIS!

The Cup Game

- Find six paper or plastic cups. Write one of these letters on the bottom of each cup: **a, b, m, n, p, t**. (Write the vowel **a** in red. Write the consonants **b, m, n, p, t** in black.)
- Place the **a** in between two of the consonants. Sound out the word. Is it a real word? Rearrange the letters to make as many words as you can.
- **JUST FOR FUN**: Stack the cups the way Alexander stacks them in the book!

FOR MORE ACTIVITIES, go to Alexander Anteater's website: www.kanepress.com / AnimalAntics / AlexanderAnteater You'll also find a recipe for Alexander Anteater's Fruit Cups!